W9-ADL-577

cloverleaf books™

Where I Live

This Is My Town

Lisa Bullard

illustrated by Paula Becker

M MILLBROOK PRESS · MINNEAPOLIS

For Mary and Minneapolis

Millbrook Press
A division of Lerner Publishing Group, Inc.
241 First Avenue North
Minneapolis, MN 55401 USA

For reading levels and more information, look up this title at
www.lernerbooks.com.

Main body text set in Slappy Inline 18/28.
Typeface provided by T26.

Library of Congress Cataloging-in-Publication Data

Names: Bullard, Lisa author. | Becker, Paula, 1958- illustrator.
Title: This is my town / by Lisa Bullard ; illustrator Paula Becker.
Description: Minneapolis : Millbrook Press, 2016. | Series:
    Cloverleaf books where i live | Includes bibliographical
    references and index.
Identifiers: LCCN 2015035606| ISBN 9781467795227
    (lb : alk. paper) | ISBN 9781467797412 (pb : alk. paper) |
    ISBN 9781467797429 (eb pdf)
Subjects: LCSH: Cities and towns—Juvenile literature.
Classification: LCC HT152 .B84 2016 | DDC 307.76—dc23

LC record available at http://lccn.loc.gov/2015035606

Manufactured in the United States of America
1 – BP – 7/15/16

TABLE OF CONTENTS

One Big Problem

My soccer team is the best! We don't always win our games. But we collected more food for the food shelf than any other group. So the mayor invited us to be in a big parade!

RIVERDALE CITY H

Mayor

clap! clap! clap! clap! clap! clap! clap! clap! cla clap!

The parade is for the birthday of our town, Riverdale. I'm so excited, but I have a big problem. We're supposed to ride our bikes in the parade. And I don't know how to ride a bike!

Urban areas are places with many buildings and people. Towns are urban areas that have a government. The mayor is the leader of the town government.

Dad says he will teach me to ride a bike, and
Grandma sent me money to buy one. All my friends
can do it. But I'm so scared to try. What if I fall?

"I'll help you practice, Rachel," says Dad. "If you're still afraid on parade day, you don't have to ride."

"I really want to ride with my team," I say. "And it's the town's birthday! Bring on the bike!"

Chapter Two

The Perfect Town for Me

I love Riverdale for so many reasons. The library has all my favorite books. There's a museum with real dinosaur bones. There's even a candy shop across the river!

I think Riverdale should have the best birthday parade ever. But riding a bike sounds scarier than meeting a real dinosaur!

Towns have schools, businesses, and homes. There are many places to meet people and have fun.

One of my cousins lives in a huge city. When I go to see him, I love riding the train. We go to baseball games and movies.

Bigger towns are called cities. Small towns are often in rural areas out in the country.

My other cousins live in a really small town. We like to play outside when I visit.

I like visiting other towns, but Riverdale is the place for me. I want to ride in its parade!

Chapter Three

Bike Day

Today is a big day. I'm getting a bike! First, Dad and I drive to the bank downtown where I save all my money from Grandma.

Then Dad drives to the store. I choose to buy the pink bike and a yellow helmet. "The helmet will help keep you safe," Dad says. "And so will a bike safety class."

The area known as downtown often has many businesses and office buildings.

We load the bike into the car and head to a bike safety class. On the way, Dad points out the new city hall building. A firefighter waves from the station next door.

"Firefighters are really brave," I say. "I bet she isn't afraid to ride a bike."

"You're brave too," says Dad. "Doing something that scares you takes a lot of courage!"

Dad pulls into the parking lot of the police station. A group of kids are gathered around a police officer. "Here's how to be a safe rider," the officer says. "Always wear your helmet so you don't get hurt!"

People such as
bus drivers and
garbage collectors help
keep a town running.
Towns also have helpers
like police officers
and firefighters.

I have almost everything I need. I have a bike and a helmet.

I have Dad to help me. I have two weeks before the parade to practice.

And I have a very special town's birthday to celebrate. Riverdale needs me!

Dad helps me get started, and we're off!
Before I know it, I'm riding all by myself!

Chapter Four
Happy Birthday, Riverdale!

What a great day for a parade! I'm so glad I learned to ride a bike. As it turns out, it's really fun. And now that I can ride, Dad says we'll explore new parts of town.

Try it: Town Map Hunt

Rachel and her dad went all over town to prepare for the parade. Can you find the places they saw on the map of Riverdale below? Can you find these same places in the story's pictures too?

- the bank
- the bike shop
- the city hall
- the police station

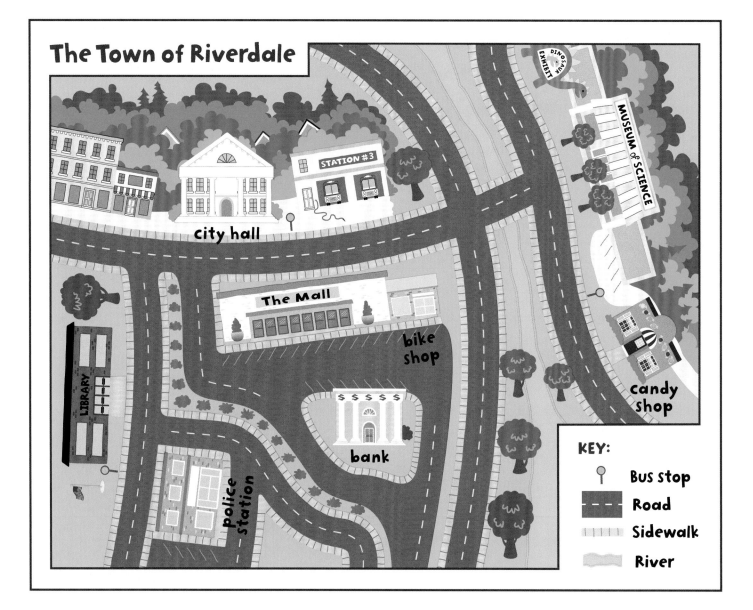

GLOSSARY

business: a company that sells items or services to make money

city: a large town

city hall: the building for a town's or city's government offices

downtown: the main business center of a town

food shelf: a place that gives food to people who can't afford to buy it

government: a set of rules that a group must live by and the people who make those rules

mayor: the town leader

rural: far from big cities and with fewer people and buildings

town: an urban area with a name and a government

urban: places with many buildings and people

Harris, Nicholas. *A Day in a City*. Minneapolis: Millbrook, 2009. Spend a whole day in a city and watch what changes from morning to night.

Jakubiak, David. *What Does a Mayor Do?* New York: Rosen, 2010. Find out more about how a mayor works in city government.

Winters, Kay. *Pete & Gabby: The Bears Go to Town*. Chicago: Albert Whitman, 2012. Read the funny story of what happens when two bear cubs visit a town.

WEBSITES

City of Westerville: Public Safety
http://ftp.westerville.org/modules/showdocument.aspx?documentid=712
Finish the word search to learn more about the work done by the police and fire departments of Westerville, Ohio.

Lakeville Kids & Government
http://www.ci.lakeville.mn.us/index.php?option=com_content&view=article&id=792&Itemid=1205
Press the word *PLAYLIST* in the upper-left corner of the video box on this website. That will show you a list of video episodes that you can watch to learn about what happens in one Minnesota town.

LERNER *e* SOURCE™
Expand learning beyond the printed book. Download free, complementary educational resources for this book from our website, www.lerneresource.com.